A Good Hare Day

Reimagining Aesop's Fable
The Hare and the Tortoise --
The Sequel

A Good Hare Day

Reimagining Aesop's Fable
The Hare and the Tortoise.
The Sequel

Written by
Craig Westover

Illustrated by
Susan Anderson

IdleTheme Press
Green Cove Springs, FL * 2023

IdleTheme Press

411 Walnut St. #10614
Green Cove Springs, FL 32043

This first edition is independently published by IdleTheme Press and printed by Amazon Kindle Direct Publishing. Artwork scans by Premier Digital & Print, Brunswick, Georgia.

ISBN: 9798376815182

A retelling of Aesop's fable *The Hare and the Tortoise** in which the Tortoise is challenged to a rematch race by an impudent Young Hare. Will this new challenger prevail and destroy the age-old moral *Slow and Steady Wins the Race*? Or does the Tortoise have a clever plan up his shell to once again defeat a hare in a race? There is always more to the story.

**The Hare and the Tortoise* adapted from *Aesop's Fables: A New Translation* by V.S. Vernon Jones with illustrations by Arthur Rackham (1912).

For "The Boys" -- Cassius, Adam, and Henry.
Remember: "There is always more to the story."
~ Craig Westover

For Brent Anderson and Tam Westover in thanks for their
patience with the endless chattering over the appropriate
expression for a tortoise.
~ Susan Anderson

A Hare was making fun of a Tortoise for being so slow upon his feet.

"Wait a bit," said the Tortoise. "I'll run a race with you, and I'll wager that I win."

"Oh, well," replied the Hare, who was much amused at the idea. "Let's try and see," he laughed.

When the course was set and the race began, both started together, but the Hare was soon so far ahead that he thought he might as well have a rest, so down he lay and fell fast asleep. Meanwhile, the Tortoise kept plodding on toward the finish line.

At last, the Hare woke up with a start and dashed at his fastest but he was too little too late. The Tortoise ambled across the finish line just ahead of the defeated Hare.

The Moral of the Story: Slow and steady wins the race.*

But, is there more to the story?

Table of Contents

CHAPTER V

> *In which the Scheme of the Tortoise appears to be working. The Hare struggles to finish the Race. He ultimately collapses and begs for Aid from the Tortoise.*

CHAPTER VI

> *In which the Rules of the Race are interpreted and a Winner is declared. A Moral Lesson is learned.*

A Literary Trailer from IdleTheme Press for ...

Reimagining Aesop's Fable *The Boy Who Cried "Wolf"*

List of Illustrations

Chapter I

Chapter II

Chapter III

Chapter IV

Chapter V

Chapter VI

Preface: A Note to Readers

A Good Hare Day is, first and foremost, a fun story about intriguing characters resolving an intense conflict. While a good story leaves the reader satisfied, the best stories leave readers speculating about events and consequences. They want more and imagine there is *more to the story*. Whether we are students, educators, aspiring writers, or casual readers, stories that stir our curiosity stay with us long after the last page is turned. These are stories that we may physically close the book on but continue to hector us with questions and what-ifs.

Rewarding reads have ideas and themes buried within them unknown even to the author -- revelations that readers discover for themselves. Enjoyable stories are treasure hunts for such hidden gems. Finding hidden treasure often means looking beyond the usual places.

A Good Hare Day is much more than just a rematch race between a tortoise and a hare. For educators and parents reading with or reading to children, the book is a useful teaching tool. Consequently, the author has prepared *A Study Guide to A Good Hare Day,* which is available from the publisher, IdleTheme Press.

A Good Hare Day is one in a series of reimagined fables intended as teaching tools. The author encourages feedback from readers, educators, and parents about the content. You can contact IdleTheme Press via email at westover4@gmail.com.

And now, What if a hare and a tortoise raced a second time ….

Master Aesop, with the benediction of a smile on his face, pronounces to a congregation of students "slow and steady wins the race."

Chapter I
More to the Story

A Brief Introduction in which a Pensive Student and a Young Hare think for themselves and Question Authority.

"History belongs to the victors," so it comes as no surprise that Aesop's fable *The Hare and the Tortoise* has trudged through history extolling the testudinal virtue that slow and steady wins the race. That moral is proper and fitting -- *for a tortoise.*

On the authority of Aesop, History belongs to the Tortoise … but to whom does the future belong?

Envision Master Aesop with the benediction of a smile on his face pronouncing to a congregation of students "slow and steady wins the race," and then departing the agora to the approving murmurs of his acolytes as they nod to the slow and steady moral of the fable.

9

Now picture a solitary and pensive student standing apart from the crowd -- a student whose mind is not bound to the tyranny of a neatly bundled morality tale. She is thinking to herself, *Might not there be more to the story?*

Indeed, there is more to the story, for on the day of that historic race between the slow and steady Tortoise and the boastful and bullying Hare, a young Hare sits on a tree stump while the disgraced and receding line of hares slinks in humiliation into the woods. He watches as the fickle forest creatures sing to the glory of the Tortoise -- their new conquering overlord. The young Hare also thinks there is more to the events of the day than meets the eye.

Why should History award virtue to the Tortoise for simply doing what a tortoise does? ponders the solitary young Hare. Slow and steady is what is seen; unseen is that slow and steady is the best the Tortoise can do. The Tortoise, like the boastful and bullying Hare, was running as fast as he could.

The Tortoise's victory is an exception, not the rule. The Tortoise did not *win* the race; the Hare *lost* the race when he arrogantly stopped to nap before finishing the race. The Tortoise did not snatch victory from the jaws of defeat; the Hare let slip defeat from the jaws of victory.

A young Hare, dejected by his fellow hare's humiliating defeat, sits pondering on a tree stump...

11

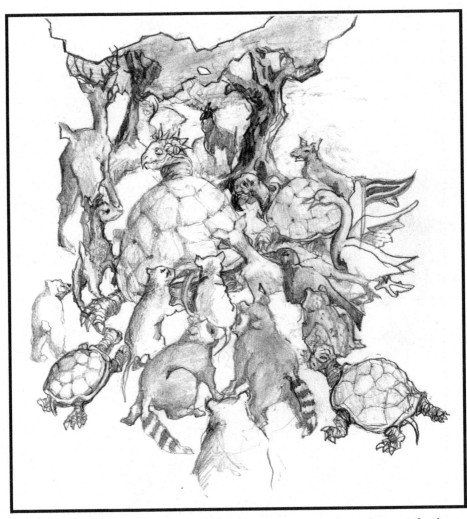

... as the fickle forest creatures sing to the glory of the Tortoise -- their new conquering overlord.

All things being equal, no slow and steady tortoise can ever defeat a swiftly running hare. No. Never. Not ever. I am so ashamed, thought the young Hare. I must avenge the boastful and bullying, the arrogant Hare's humiliating defeat. History must know that any hare can outrun any tortoise any day of the week.

The young Hare leaped upon the tree stump.

"Wait!"

The Young Hare leaped upon the tree stump ...

Chapter II
The Challenge

In which the Young Hare challenges the Tortoise to a Rematch Race, and the Tortoise evokes the Rules to avoid the immediate Challenge.

"Wait!"

The procession of forest creatures, mindlessly marching at a slow and steady pace behind the victorious Tortoise, nonetheless bumped into and tripped over each other when the Tortoise stopped without warning. Flanked by his fellow tortoises and surrounded by the fawning forest creatures, the Tortoise slowly stomped around in a half-circle to face the Hare. All eyes focused on the Tortoise and the Hare.

"Yeeeeeeesss?" The Tortoise stared in annoyance at such an impudent Hare.

"I challenge you to a rematch race," said the young Hare.

"And what makes you think the results would be any different?" was the measured response of the Tortoise.

"Because all things being equal any hare can outrun any tortoise any day of the week," replied the Hare.

"Not this day," said the Tortoise. "Not on this day. Not in this place. Not at this time. Do you not believe in miracles?"

"Not on this day. Not in this place. Not at this time."

"I do not." The Hare thumped his lucky foot for emphasis.

"I do not believe that an event as rare as a black swan deserves royal adoration. Today's race was just a bad hare

16

day. Nothing more. Slow and steady may have its place, but that place is not on a racecourse. All things being equal, a hare will always outrun a tortoise. I will outrun you or any champion tortoise you might choose. I do not believe in miracles. I believe in myself."

The Tortoise rotated his huge head from side to side. From inside his shell, he pulled a long scroll. He shook it in the face of the Hare.

"I believe the Rules of the race are quite clear," he enunciated slowly. "One race *per annum*. Winner takes all. The Rules *explicitly* state there can be but one race per year. So, I *will* agree to race you -- *exactly* one year from today. I suggest you take it slow and steady until that day."

"We could just as easily race now."

The Tortoise solemnly shook his head. "No. Rules are Rules, and Rules must be obeyed *explicitly*. And it would hardly be … ahem … as you say 'equal' for this tired old tortoise to compete against a fresh young hare. It is not easy dragging a heavy shell through the forest. And it will be good for you hares to learn some humility. *Slow and steady wins the race.* Ponder that wisdom, my furry friend."

"Rules are Rules, and Rules must be obeyed explicitly."

A murmur of agreement rippled through the congregation of forest creatures. Again stomping in a half-circle, the Tortoise turned his massive shell to the Hare. He flicked a little dirt with his hind legs as he ambled away.

"Hare today. Gone tomorrow," he mumbled. The creep of tortoises and the mob of forest creatures fell in line behind the Tortoise and paraded triumphantly, albeit slow and steady, into the forest.

Chapter III
Training and Scheming

A Year passes in which the Hardworking Hare trains while the Tortoise schemes for Advantage in the Rematch Race.

And so it was that the young Hare, ignoring the "slow and steady" advice of the Tortoise, leaped into daily training. He ran great distances never stopping to rest. He ran in all kinds of weather -- under the blistering sun, in rain and snow and sleet, on dry and hard cracked ground, and through heavy mud. He practiced leaping over tree limbs and branches. He even hopped on three legs on the off chance he were injured during the race. He prepared for anything and everything. Almost anything and everything.

Every day the Hare trained, and every day the fickle forest creatures lined his route to jeer and mock him. "Slow and steady," they shouted and laughed. "Don't you need a nap about now?"

The Hare ignored the taunts. He continued his training alone until one day, several months into his regimen, another hare ran behind him. A few days later, the Second Hare was joined by another. A few days later three more hares joined

Every day the Hare trained, and every day the fickle forest creatures lined his route to jeer and mock him.

in the training. Soon a large drove of hares raced through the forest in all kinds of weather -- under the blistering sun, in rain and snow and sleet, on dry and hard cracked ground, and through heavy mud. In synchronized waves, the drove of hares leaped over tree limbs and branches.

As the number of hares increased, the mob of taunters shrank away. Most of the forest creatures simply stopped showing up for the daily Hare-mocking, but a few of the

Soon a large drove of hares raced through the forest in all kinds of weather ...

more speedy creatures (who only pretended to accept, but never really bought into, the slow and steady mantra) joined in the training. Soon, the only daily observer of the Hare's determination was a Wise Old Tortoise tucked in his shell hiding among the trees beside the path.

The Wise Old Tortoise swayed his head from side to side as the Hare bounded past his hidden vantage point, followed by wave upon wave of leaping hares, followed by

The only daily observer of the Hare's determination was a Wise Old Tortoise tucked in his shell among the trees.

rambunctious and laughing forest creatures. When the last of the forest creatures passed, the Wise Old Tortoise ambled, slow and steady, back to the sandpit where the overlord Tortoise lay in the sun surrounded by his creep, thoroughly enjoying his newly minted status and power.

"Where have you been?" The Tortoise looked up from a copy of the Rules of the race he had been studiously perusing.

22

The Tortoise looked up from a copy of the Rules of the race he had been studiously perusing.

"Watching the Hare train."

"Weeeeeeelll?"

"This is a hungry hare," said the Wise Old Tortoise. "He runs great distances never stopping to rest. He runs in all kinds of weather -- under the blistering sun, in rain and snow and sleet, on dry and hard cracked ground, and through heavy mud. He practices leaping over tree limbs and branches. He

23

even hops on three legs on the off chance he were injured. He is prepared for anything and everything. He inspires hope among the hares. He excites the creatures of the forest. We must watch out for this one. We may need another miracle."

The overlord Tortoise stretched his neck and elevated his head high above his colossal shell.

"Promising miracles keeps the creep and the forest creatures in awe of me," said the Tortoise. "The fickle forest creatures do not like responsibility and hard work. They prefer hope and miracles. Whether by cunning or luck, if I happen to provide a "miracle" for them, well, so much the better for me."

The Tortoise glanced down at the Rules of the race spread out on the sand at his feet.

"Like the Hare, I believe in myself but in a different way," he said. "The Hare says, "All things being equal, any hare will outrun any tortoise."" The Tortoise smiled a cunning smile. "We shall see. We shall see."

Chapter IV
Rules are Rules

In which the Cunning of the Tortoise is revealed, and the Hare learns that Rules are Rules and must be obeyed **explicitly***.*

Three hundred and sixty-five times had rosy-fingered Dawn Homerically blossomed in the eastern sky when the forest creatures gathered once again to witness a race between a tortoise and a hare.

On one side of the clearing, patiently awaiting the arrival of their overlord, sat supporters of the Tortoise. Across the glade, surrounded by the drove of hares and a good number of fickle forest creatures, the Hare bounced up and down, loosening up, psyching himself for the race.

"Carpe diem! Carpe diem! Carpe diem!" vigorously chanted the hares and their supporters. "Seize the day! Seize the day!"

"Slow and steady …. Slow and steady…. Slow and steady" came a more measured and subdued response from the supporters of the Tortoise, a chant that diminished further in enthusiasm as the explicitly appointed time for the start of the race approached.

The forest creatures supporting the Tortoise began to shift nervously and murmur among themselves wondering if the weather might not be too hot for the Tortoise and casting about to see which way the wind was blowing. They kept their eyes on the forest path. Racing through their minds was the nagging thought that maybe the "miracle" victory of the Tortoise was, as the Hare said, a serendipitous black swan event. The young Hare might be right: Any hare *can* outrun any tortoise any day of the week. On this day, at this time, in this place, there would be no miracle.

Perhaps the same thought trudged through the mind of the Tortoise. Perhaps the Tortoise would not show up for the race and leave his victory unchallenged. Perhaps a miracle should not be challenged too vigorously lest it proves more fortuitous than miraculous.

Suddenly, the ground began to rumble. The bushes began to shake. The creep of tortoises, the reigning champion and forest overlord Tortoise in the lead, trudged into the clearing, their massive shells reflecting emerald green in the sunlight.

The Tortoise marched slowly but steadily up to the Hare.

"Well....well," said the Tortoise. "Here we are again."

"Yes, and ready to go." The Hare hopped back and forth on his back paws. "This year, the race will not take long."

Suddenly, the ground began to rumble. The bushes began to shake.

"Carpe diem!" shouted the hares.

The Tortoise looked over at the hares and the fickle forest creatures that had joined them. He noticed a few more of his supporters surreptitiously sneak around the clearing to stand behind the hares.

"I have been thinking about what you said." The Tortoise addressed the Hare. "All things being equal, perhaps a hare might outrun a tortoise. If you are correct, all things being equal, this day might well indeed result in an ignominious defeat."

"You're backing out of the race? You are conceding victory?" The Hare was puzzled. From the drove of hares came a rather poor but recognizable imitation of clucking chickens.

"No, no," said the Tortoise. "I am not withdrawing. However reluctantly, I will race you. All things being equal, I am honor-bound to go through with the race." He stared at the Hare. "As are you?"

"Of course," said the Hare. "It is not my intent to humiliate you. I merely want to set the record right. It is what it is: Any hare *can* outrun any tortoise any day of the week."

"All things being equal?" asked the Tortoise.

"All things being equal," agreed the Hare.

"Very well. All things being equal." The Tortoise turned to one of his companions. "I shall make myself equal to a hare." With that, a pretty young tortoise to his right reached into her shell and pulled out a fluffy white ball of milkweed and cottonwood seeds. She affixed the fluffy ball to the rear end of the overlord Tortoise's massive shell.

28

"All things being equal … I shall make myself equal to a hare."

"I never did understand the purpose of the little ball of fluff on a hare's rear end, but," the Tortoise shrugged, "all things being equal …."

Meanwhile, the handsome young tortoise on his overlord's left pulled from his shell two long white feathers of the kind molted by birds in the forest. These he attached like a hare's ears to the head of the Tortoise, much to the amusement of the hares.

"The stupid Tortoise thinks that a fluffy seed tail and feather ears will make him run like a hare," shouted one of the hares. "Stupid, stupid Tortoise," declared another.

All the hares laughed. Even some of the forest creatures joined in mocking the Tortoise. A few more noted which way the wind was blowing and slid over to join the Hare's supporters.

The Hare only smiled. "You make quite the … a … err …um … quite the handsome hare," he said. "All things now being equal, no doubt you will run like the wind. Now, let the race begin." The Hare hopped toward the starting line.

"Waaaait!"

The Hare stopped in his tracks.

"All things are not equal." The Tortoise motioned with his head. His feather ears fluttered in the breeze. From the back of the creep, two muscular tortoises struggled to haul forward an empty but very heavy tortoise shell.

"I have done my best to make myself equal to a hare," said the Tortoise. "Is it not fair that you should make yourself equal to a tortoise?" The Tortoise lifted one front leg and pointed to the feather ears on his head. He shook his massive shell and wiggled his fluffy tail.

The hares shouted in protest.

Two muscular tortoises struggled to haul forward an empty but very heavy tortoise shell.

"But this is not *equal*," said the Hare. "It is not what I meant. 'All things being equal' means each of us is free to run as fast as we can to decide who is the fastest runner. 'Equality' does not mean turning a tortoise into a hare and a hare into a tortoise."

"Oh," said the Tortoise. "Well, perhaps I may have misunderstood what you meant by 'all things being equal,' but the Rules of the race -- and Rules must be obeyed

31

explicitly -- clearly state that the victor establishes the Rules of the race. I am the victor. The Rules mean what I say they mean -- *explicitly*. The Rules for this race state 'all things being equal.' This means I will do my best to be a hare, and you will take on the characteristics of a tortoise. I shall wear the fluffy tail and big ears of a hare; you must (as the Rules say) 'hop a mile in my shell.' I stand for the Sacred Principle of Equality under the Rules. Surely, you do not stand against the Sacred Principle of Equality?"

Rules being Rules, and with the eyes of all the creatures of the forest staring at him, the Hare nodded his head in submission. He could not stand against the Sacred Principle of Equality, so he stood still while the two muscular tortoises strapped the heavy tortoiseshell to his back. The Hare's legs were cramped inside the shell and his paws barely extended past the bottom of the shell. His ears were pinned inside the shell where it rode over his neck.

Training for the race the idealistic Hare had run great distances never stopping to rest. He ran in all kinds of weather -- under the blistering sun, in rain and snow and sleet, on dry and hard cracked ground, and through heavy mud. He practiced leaping over tree limbs and branches. He even hopped on three legs on the off chance he were injured

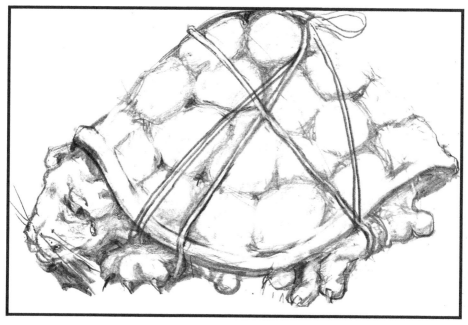

"You must (as they say) 'Hop a mile in my shell.'"

during the race. He prepared for anything and everything -- anything and everything except craft and cunning.

The Tortoise ambled over to the starting line. His feather ears fluttered as he moved, and his fluffy seed tail bounced up and down. "Well, we're ready to get this race underway. A mile-and-a-quarter is a long way to run. We do want to finish before dark."

The Hare tried to bound to the starting line, but his feet never left the ground; he fell but a few inches forward. He tried again. He fell again.

"Slow and steady," said the Tortoise, smirking. "Slow and steady. One foot at a time."

Moving one foot at a time, slow and steady, the Hare crawled to the starting line.

"Let the race begin!" The Tortoise nodded to a raven perched on a tree branch above the starting line. The raven squawked. The race was on.

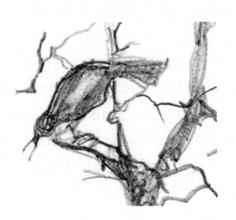

Chapter V
Race Redux

In which the Scheme of the Tortoise appears to be working. The Hare struggles to finish the race. He ultimately collapses and begs for Aid from the Tortoise.

As in the original Aesop's fable *The Hare and the Tortoise,* there is little need for a long and boring description of a slow and steady race. It is enough to say the Hare made a valiant effort while laboring under the burden of the heavy tortoise shell. He kept pace with the Tortoise -- at times he even pulled slightly ahead. But after hours of struggle cramped in the heavy shell, just in sight of the finish line, at the exact spot where the year before the boastful and bullying Hare had paused to nap, less than a quarter-mile from the finish line, the exhausted Hare collapsed.

The Tortoise, who held a slight lead in the race stopped, turned, and arrogantly ambled back to the collapsed Hare. "Slow and steady wins the race," chuckled the heavy-footed Tortoise as he plodded up to the prone and exhausted Hare.

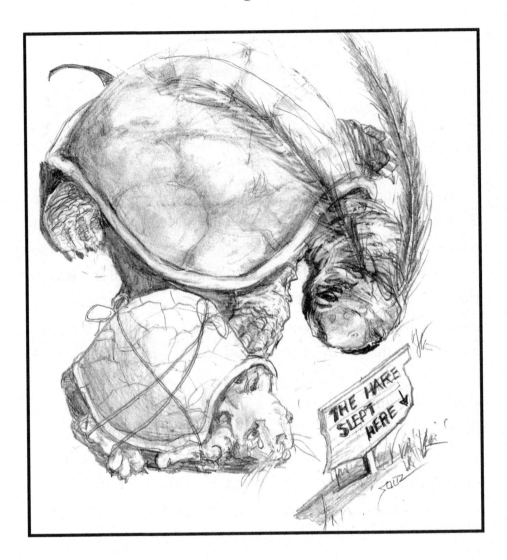

"Slow and steady wins the race," chuckled the heavy-footed Tortoise as he plodded up to the prone and exhausted Hare.

"All your hard work. All your training. Running great distances and never stopping to rest. Running in all kinds of weather -- under the blistering sun, in rain and snow and sleet, on dry and hard cracked ground, and through heavy mud. Leaping over tree limbs and branches. Hopping on three legs on the off chance you were injured during the race. All your preparation is undone, not by a miracle, but through *my* craft and cunning."

The Hare lay panting under the weight of the heavy tortoise shell. "Yes," he whispered, gasping for breath. "You are right. The craft and cunning of a tortoise trump the merits of the hard work of a hare. All things being equal, when a tortoise assumes the trappings of a hare and a hare bears the burden of a tortoise, a tortoise can, on any day of the week, outrun a hare. I see the error of my ways." The hare wheezed audibly, as if on his last breath.

The Tortoise scoffed and turned to amble off toward the finish line.

"Wait," gasped the Hare.

The Tortoise paused and stomped around in a half-circle to face the all-but-defeated Hare.

"Yeeeeeeesss?"

"The heavy tortoise shell -- I don't know how you bear it

-- is resting on my neck. I can't breathe. The shell is crushing my lucky foot and has injured it painfully. Before you race off and claim your victory, can you loosen the straps on the heavy shell? Just a little so I can breathe? I am too weak to finish the race, let alone cast off this heavy shell, and the Rules explicitly state I must 'run a mile in your shell.'"

The Tortoise laughed. "Of course. My charity only adds to the ignominy of your defeat. History belongs to the victors, and History will sing of the craft and cunning of the Tortoise and of his charity in victory."

The Tortoise loosened the straps binding the gasping Hare pinned in the heavy tortoise shell. He gave it a slight nudge, freeing the Hare's front foot.

"Lucky for you I am so charitable that I nudged the shell off your 'lucky' foot," mocked the Tortoise.

"Thank you," sighed the Hare. "But I thump my own luck," he whispered softly.

The Tortoise turned and, slow and steady, ambled toward the finish line. A growing murmur slowly rising to a cheer echoed through the forest. Tortoises stretched their necks and waved their heads triumphantly. Fickle forest creatures no longer doubted miracles. All the while, the slow and steady Tortoise plodded forward.

A Good Hare Day

"Slow and steady….Slow and Steady…..Slow and Steady."

Hare today. Gone tomorrow, thought the Tortoise. He was but a few yards from the finish line.

Suddenly, the forest went quiet. The forest creatures gaped with open, silent mouths, and then a cheer rose from the drove of hares that cascaded into a thunderous roar. Forest creatures dashed across the clearing to join them.

"Carpe Diem! Carpe DIEM! CARPE DIEM!

The Tortoise turned his head just in time to see the Hare, holding his lucky foot tightly against his chest, hopping on three legs, bound past him, and by a hair's breadth, the Hare stretched across the finish line in front of him.

The hares leaped about, thumping their legs. Forest creatures squawked, squeaked, and howled. Tortoises grunted angrily. Glowering, the Tortoise stalked across the finish line and marched directly up to the victorious Hare.

The Hare, holding his lucky foot tightly against his chest, hopping on three legs, stretched past the Tortoise.

Chapter VI
The Moral of the Story

In which the Rules of the Race are interpreted and a Winner is declared. A Moral Lesson is learned.

"You cheated," grunted the Tortoise. "You broke the Rules. You shed the shell of a tortoise. All things were not equal."

"To the contrary," said the Hare, "I followed the Rules -- your Rules as you demanded, I followed them *explicitly*. I was to 'hop a mile in your shell.' In fact, I hopped *more* than a mile in your shell. Did you forget the race course was a mile-and-a-quarter long? Plus, I took on even more characteristics of a tortoise. I used the craft and cunning of a tortoise to get free of the heavy shell. Surely, my craft and cunning make me equal to a tortoise -- *explicitly* on this day, at this time, in this place. All things being equal, *I* snatched victory from the jaws of defeat. *I* won the race. Indeed, it is a good hare day."

"That's not what I meant," stammered the Tortoise. "I was to wear the fluffy tail and feather ears of a hare for the entire race; you were to bear the burden of a heavy tortoise shell for the entire race -- not just a mile."

"Ponder this lesson well, my hard-shelled friend ..."

"Oh," said the Hare. "Well, perhaps I misunderstood what you meant by 'all things being equal,' but I *explicitly* obeyed the Rules agreed to and the Rules stated, *explicitly,* I must 'hop a mile in your shell.' The Rules meant what you said they meant -- *explicitly.*"

The Hare hopped up on the stump in the center of the clearing and stared into the eyes of the Tortoise.

"Ponder this lesson well, my hard-shelled friend: *Craft and cunning cannot make a tortoise into a hare nor a hare into a tortoise. In the long run, craft and cunning alone cannot defeat hard work and preparation. Craft and cunning may fool History, but hard work and preparation make History. The future belongs to the hares.*"

The Hare smiled a cunning smile.

"You declared that you honorably stood for the Sacred Principle of Equality under the Rules. Surely you will not now deny the Sacred Principle of Equality?"

Watching the exchange between the Tortoise and the Hare, the ever-fickle forest creatures murmured in support of the Hare. The Tortoise grunted. He turned without a word. The disgraced and deposed Tortoise slunk off into the woods among the creep of humiliated tortoises.

Indeed, Aesop's fable of *The Hare and the Tortoise* is more than a simple morality tale. History may be fooled into belonging to Aesop's slow and steady Tortoise, but the future will be made by pensive students and hard-working hares, thinking for themselves, and constantly questioning authority.

The Moral of the Story: *There is always more to any story.*

IdleTheme Press

If we shadows have offended,
Think but this, and all is mended,
That you have but slumber'd here
While these visions did appear.
*And this weak and **idle theme**,*
No more yielding but a dream.
~~ from A Midsummer Night's Dream by William Shakespeare

Thank you for reading *A Good Hare Day*. If you enjoyed this sequel to Aesop's Fable *The Hare and the Tortoise*, you might like other reimagined fables from IdleTheme Press -- *There is always more to any story.*

Next up for publication is *Drinking Beer and Telling Lies*, which reveals the back story of *The Boy Who Cried "Wolf."* Is there more to the story than the simple moral: *Liars will not be rewarded; even if they tell the truth, no one believes them*? Watch for the future publication of *Drinking Beer and Telling Lies* to learn the answer.

Added Value: IdleTheme Press offers study guides for each of its reimagined fables. To purchase a study guide or for information about bulk purchases for educational institutions, email the author at westover4@gmail.com or contact:

IdleTheme Press
411 Walnut St. #10614
Green Cove Springs, FL 32043

A Literary Trailer for the IdleTheme Press Publication ...

Drinking Beer and Telling Lies

Reimagining Aesop's Fable
The Boy Who Cried "Wolf."

Anthony the shepherd boy was bored. Anthony was not bored in the sense he had nothing to do; Anthony was bored in the sense that all he had to do amounted to nothing.

Day after day, just as the sun tickled the sky into a fresh pinkness, Anthony urged and prodded the flock of sheep from the fold. He herded them to the pastureland bordered by the dense forest on the side of the mountain just outside the town. Day after day, as the sun trudged across the sky, Anthony sat in the shade of a tree playing his shepherd's pipe or whittling at sticks while his dog kept the flock together. Day after day, as the sun hurried on its travels to the nether parts of the globe, Anthony herded the sheep along the familiar path back down the mountain and into the Village fold from which he had led them that morning and from which they would depart on the morrow.

Night after night, month after month, in darkness and moonlight, his day's work done, Anthony sat on the ground in the doorway of his small hut from where he could hear laughter and jocularity wafting like the aroma of roasting mutton from the *Huntsman's Horn,* the town tavern, where, at any hour day or night, villagers and huntsmen gathered to drink beer and tell lies.

"What exciting lives the huntsmen lead," mused Anthony. He fingered his own huntsman's horn, fashioned from the horn of a ram, that hung from the belt of his tunic. Given to him by the Village Headmaster, his huntsman's horn was Anthony's most prized possession.

"A huntsman's horn is a grave responsibility," the Headmaster told Anthony. "Should a wolf threaten the flock, blow the horn, and villagers and huntsmen will come running to your aid."

In his early days as the Village shepherd, Anthony took his responsibility most seriously. With his faithful dog at his side, with one hand on his huntsman's horn and the other on a sharpened tree branch, ever alert for the sign of a wolf, Anthony patrolled around the grazing flock. But as the days of vigilance withered into days of routine, Anthony grew restless, and his restlessness proved more fatiguing than patrolling the flock. The dog did the work keeping the sheep herded together; Anthony sat in the shade of a tree thinking of nothing in particular -- until he heard the far-off but nonetheless clear blast of a huntsman's horn.

HMMMMMMMMmmmmmmmmmmmmmmmmmmmmmm mmmmmmmmmmm.........

The huntsmen are driving game, thought Anthony. Or perhaps they have cornered a wolf.

More horns blared in a cacophony of wails, the sound growing louder as the unseen huntsmen converged, until one mighty blast, a harmonious, single-note symphony signaled a successful hunt.

HMMMMMMMMMmmmmmmmmmmmmmmmmmmmmmm mmmmmmmmmmm.........

"What exciting lives the huntsmen lead," sighed Anthony.

And so passed another day. The sun trudged across the sky until it reached its zenith then slid rapidly towards the horizon and hurried on its travels to the nether parts of the globe. Anthony herded the sheep along the familiar path back down the mountain and into the fold from which he had led them that morning and from which he would lead them on the morrow. The flock in the fold, his day's work done, Anthony sat on the ground in the doorway of his small hut from where he could hear laughter and jocularity wafting like the aroma of roasting mutton from the *Huntsman's Horn* where villagers and huntsmen were gathered drinking beer and telling lies.

Rubbing the huntsman's horn at his belt, Anthony stood up, brushed the dust from his tunic, and with small, hesitant steps made his way towards the *Huntsman's Horn*. Anthony never actually patronized the tavern. He never tried to join in the comradery of the villagers and huntsmen. He simply walked down to the tavern and sat outside; Anthony crouched beside the sidewall of the tavern and peered in through a window.

The *Huntsman's Horn* was packed with villagers and huntsmen. Some sat around tables, and others stood at the bar. In the center of the room, standing atop a table and waving a flagon of beer, a bawdy, brawny huntsman, a massive arm about the waist of a buxom barmaid, held the focus of villagers and his fellow huntsmen.

"Did you ever see a larger or more ferocious wolf?" The huntsman raised his glass to his comrades leaning against the bar. "Why he was five feet at the shoulders if he were an inch. Two hundred pounds if he were an ounce."

"The wolf was 30 inches at the shoulders when you killed it," shouted a huntsman at the bar.

"And 110 pounds," shouted another.

"And 40 inches and 180 pounds after I served you the fourth beer," giggled the barmaid.

"The monster grows larger by the beer," a villager chimed in.

The crowd laughed good-naturedly.

"Another beer and the dead wolf will grow another 12 inches and weigh another 50 pounds," shouted a third huntsman.

Again the crowd roared in good-natured laughter; villagers and huntsmen toasted each other. Beer glasses clinked together. Waves of beer splashed onto the tavern floor.

The huntsman atop the table laughed as hard as anyone. He slipped his arm from the barmaid's waist and pointed his finger at his friends at the bar.

"And a few more beers down your gullets, lads, and you'll all bloody believe me."

Again the crowd burst into laughter, and the bawdy, brawny huntsman joined in laughing loudest of all. He raised his glass.

"Here's to more beer," he toasted.

"And more lies," came a shout from the crowd. More laughter as the huntsman leaped from the table, lifted the buxom barmaid to the floor, kissed her full on the lips, and joined his comrades at the bar....

Drinking Beer and Telling Lies will be available soon. From **IdleTheme Press**, 411 Walnut St. #10614, Green Cove Springs, FL 32043 or by contacting the author at westover4@gmail.com.

About the Author

Craig Westover made a career of "entrepreneurial" writing. He's been a magazine writer, a copywriter, a non-fiction ghostwriter, a communications executive, a speechwriter, a think tank Senior Fellow, and an opinion page columnist for a big-city newspaper. "But," says Craig, "a writer thinks mean of himself that has never written poetry and fiction."

In 2015 Craig and his wife, Tamara, sold their home in Minnesota and retired to the 40-ft trawler IdleTheme plying the seas between Brunswick, Georgia and The Bahamas. His "weak and idle theme": To try his hand at poetry and fiction and …

To see the world in an endless sea, where heaven weds the ocean; where all you see is infinity, and time is just a notion.

About the Artist

Susan Anderson has been doodling and drawing despite frowns from authorities for many decades. "At last," she says, "I am of an age where I can have at." Illustrating *A Good Hare Day* was a fun and thought-provoking project for Susan. "In drawing my main characters for the Tortoise and the Hare, I wanted to have them show emotion without metamorphosing them. I started by using the author as my first model for the Tortoise. The Young Hare will remain anonymous."

Made in the USA
Monee, IL
24 June 2023

37174528R00036